My
Dinosaur

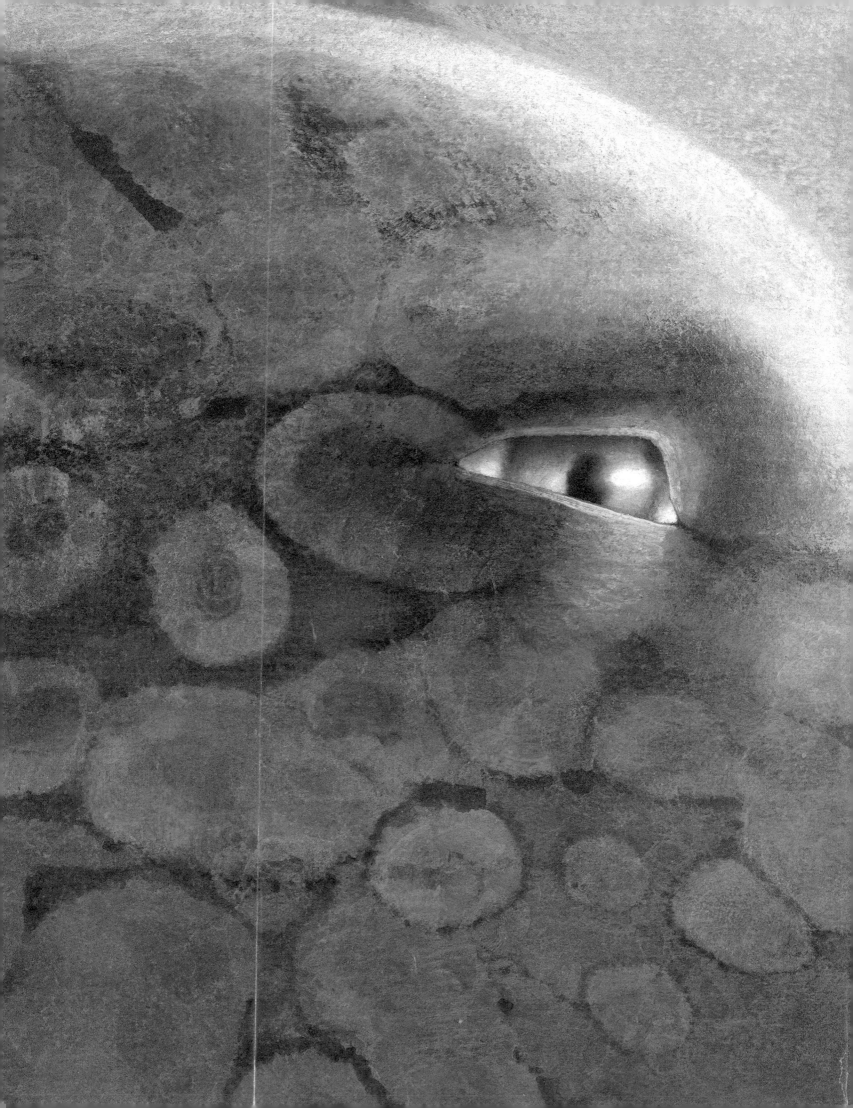

My Dinosaur

Mark Alan Weatherby

SCHOLASTIC PRESS • NEW YORK

Text copyright © 1997 by Scholastic Inc.
Illustrations copyright © 1997 by Mark Alan Weatherby.
All rights reserved. Published by Scholastic Press,
a division of Scholastic Inc., *Publishers since 1920.*

LIBRARY OF CONGRESS CATALOGING-IN-PUBLICATION DATA

Weatherby, Mark Alan.
My dinosaur / by Mark Alan Weatherby.   p. cm.
Summary: Every night a little girl waits by her
window for her friend the dinosaur. When he
comes, they play and frolic in the woods
all night until the sun comes up.

[1. Dinosaurs—Fiction.   2. Friendship—Fiction.]
I. Title   PZ7.W3534My 1997
[E]—dc20   95-42020   CIP AC

ISBN 0-590-97203-0

12 11 10 9 8 7 6 5 4 3 2 1   7 8 9/9 0 1 2/0
Printed in Singapore   46
First printing, March 1997

Book design by Marijka Kostiw

The Cheerios box on page 30 was printed
with the permission of General Mills, Inc.

The text type was set in 21 pt. Plantin Bold.
The display type was set in AT Pelican.
Mark Alan Weatherby's artwork
was rendered in acrylics,
metallic paints . . .
and fairy dust.

For my little princess, Sophi:
May all your dreams come true. . .
—M.A.W.

*L*ate at night,
when the moon is full,
I wait by the window
for my dinosaur.
Will he come tonight?

At first, I can't see him,
but I can hear him.
I look hard.
Is that his tail behind the tree?

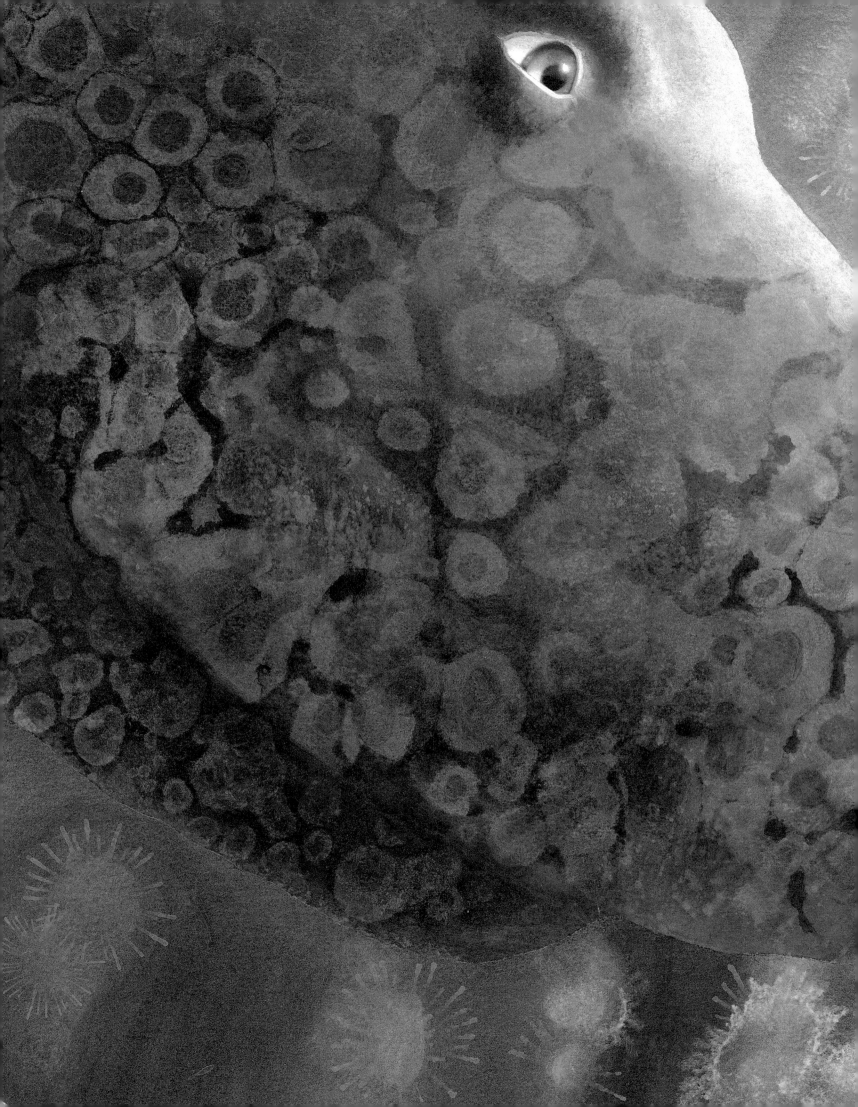

I run outside through the
dark forest and whistle.
That is our signal.
Now he knows I'm here.

My dinosaur!
First, we play hide-and-seek in the shadows.
When I find him, I tiptoe up behind him . . .
and surprise him!

Next, I climb up on his back.
We take a night ride through the forest.
My dinosaur runs so fast,
it feels like we are flying.

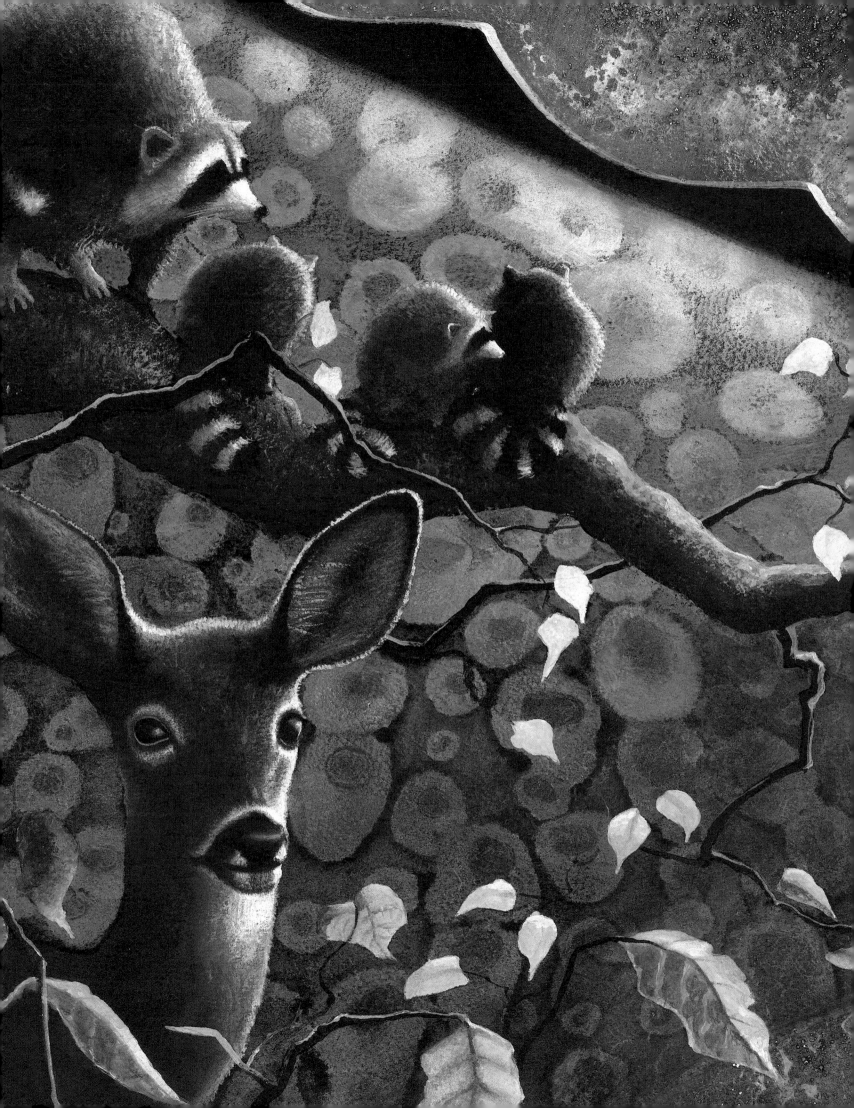

My dinosaur never scares
the night creatures.
They like him.
I wave as we race by.

When we get thirsty,
my dinosaur stops at the river.
We take a drink.

We swim in the
moonlit water.
The fish jump up to say,
"Hello!"

My dinosaur lifts me above the treetops
and stretches his neck to the sky.
I can almost reach the stars!

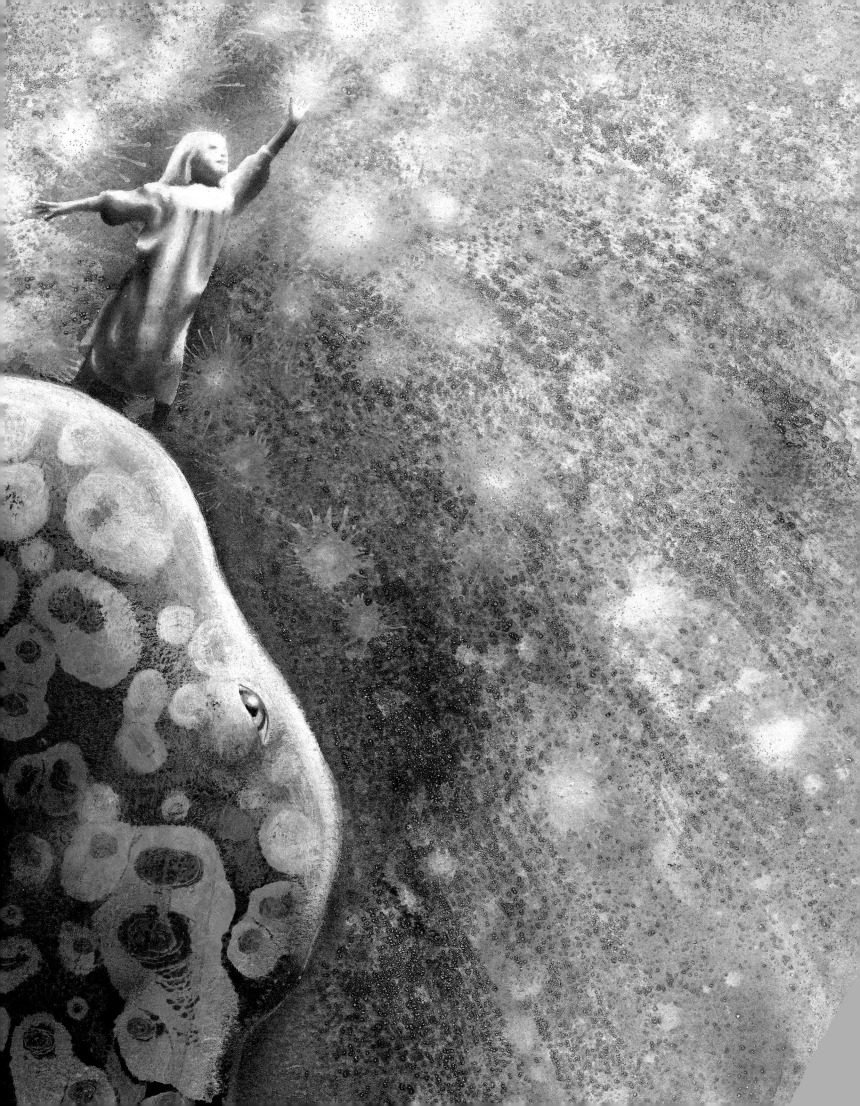

When the first rays
of the sun come up,
it's time to go.

As we gallop home,
I sing my good-bye song:

Good night, my dinosaur.
Sleep tight, my dinosaur.
Soon I'll see you again,
my very best friend.
Good night, sleep tight,
my dinosaur . . . .

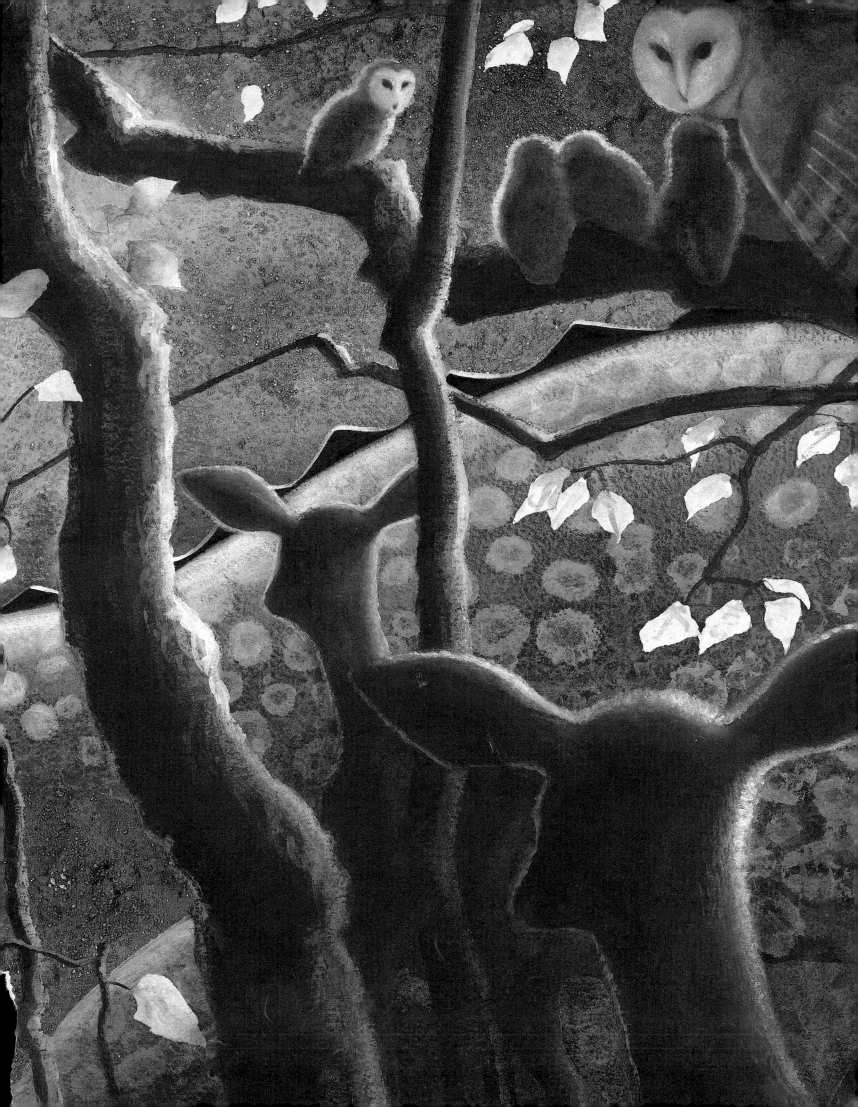

My dinosaur lifts me to my window.
He waits until I am under the covers.
Then, quiet as a mouse,
he heads for home.

At breakfast, I yawn.
"How did you get leaves in your hair?"
my mother asks me.
"I played with my dinosaur last night,"
I tell her.
"That's nice," she says.

I look outside the window
but my great, old friend is gone.
He will come back again
when the moon is full, I know. . . .
My dinosaur always does.